Tr

Published in 2012
by Wayland

Wayland
338 Euston Road
London NW1 3BH

Wayland Australia
Level 17/207 Kent Street
Sydney, NSW 2000

Series Editor: Louise John
Editor: Katie Powell
Cover design: Paul Cherrill
Design: D.R.ink
Consultant: Shirley Bickler

A CIP catalogue record for this book is available from the British Library.

ISBN 9780750263399

Printed in China

First published in 2010, reprinted in 2011, 2012, 2014.
Wayland is a division of Hachette Children's Books,
an Hachette UK Company

www.hachette.co.uk

Treasure Trail

Written by Karen Wallace
Illustrated by Jackie Harland

WAYLAND

It was a sunny morning on the farm. All the animals were eating breakfast.

"Who put this ribbon on my door?" asked Horse.

“There was some shiny ribbon
on my nest, too,” said Hen.
“Where did it come from?”

"I think that someone has given you both a present," said Dog.

"Who was it?" asked Horse and Hen.

"I'm a detective," said Dog.
"I'll find out."

Detective Dog went to see Cow.

She had a silver bell around her neck.

"Did someone give you a present, Cow?" said Dog.

"I've got a present, too," said Sheep, holding a red flower.

Then Dog saw Cat chasing a gold ball across the farmyard.

Dog began to think hard.
All the presents were small and shiny. That must be a clue!

"Magpie likes small, shiny things," said Dog. "It must be her!"

“But she’s never spoken to us,” said Cat. “Why did she give us presents?”

"That's what I'm going to find out," said Dog.

Dog set off to find Magpie.
He looked for her everywhere.
He had to find the answer.

On the way back to the farmyard, Dog saw a trail of small, shiny objects on the ground.

Dog followed the trail to a big tree. Magpie's nest was at the top!

"Hello, Magpie," called Dog.
"Did you give presents to all the animals?"

"Yes," said Magpie. "I want to make friends but I'm too shy to talk to them."

"We want to be friends with you, too" said Dog kindly. "Why don't you come and build a new nest in the farmyard?"

“Can I?” asked Magpie.
“Oh, yes, please!”

At the farmyard, all the animals rushed to meet her.

"Thank you for our presents," they cried. "We've got some for you, too!"

The animals gave Magpie some wool, some fur, some horsehair and some feathers.

Magpie began to build
a beautiful nest in
the farmyard.

"I'm so glad you found me, Dog!" said Magpie. "You're the best detective ever!"

START READING is a series of highly enjoyable books for beginner readers. **The books have been carefully graded to match the Book Bands widely used in schools.** This enables readers to be sure they choose books that match their own reading ability.

Look out for the Band colour on the book in our Start Reading logo.

The Bands are:

START READING books can be read independently or shared with an adult. They promote the enjoyment of reading through satisfying stories supported by fun illustrations.

Karen Wallace was brought up in a log cabin in Canada. She has written lots of different books for children and even won a few awards. Karen likes writing funny books because she can laugh at her own jokes! She has two sons and two cats.

Jackie Harland is woken up every morning by her two cats taking it in turns to nibble her toes and pat her face with their paws. It works every time, and they always get their breakfast first. In spite of that, she loves them very much, and after she finally gets to eat her own breakfast, she loves painting, especially animals.